Extemporaneous Automatics

Jim Ivy

All stories, artwork and design by Jim Ivy

ISBN: 979-8-218-41504-4

This book is dedicated to my family: Jennifer, Miyo and Tatum,
whose inspiration is a lifetime's worth of wealth, and to my friends and
musical partners, who have pushed me to do better. I salute you all.

Automatics are just that: immediate, single thought ideas that are flushed out on the spot until they feel complete.

I used to do this as a mental exercise to keep my imagination nimble (avoid boredom) and as a form of improvisation with ideas. I have adopted the same general concepts and "rules" in other disciplines, musical projects and solo performances.

It's a simple process and not particularly original. Much like the stream of consciousness writing techniques, an automatic is spontaneous in origination. However, unlike surrealist prose, the entire piece is not constructed this way.

That spark of an idea is then used as a basis of a completed thought or narrative, keeping in mind a sort of story-telling approach, with linear construction and architecture to convey an anecdote. This is all done within the moment, not after calculating the story or composing themes. As quickly as I can write or type it, that's how it stays. They are only revisited for the sake of grammar and spelling.

An automatic is complete when the original thought is satisfied, as one complete presentation. It doesn't necessarily have to have a conclusion or even a general concept, it just has to feel completed.

Over the years, I have used various sets of strategic guidelines with the automatics, set up as compositional stipulations, to be used as stimulation hurdles or creative challenges, rather than conceptual flourishing. They make it fun.

In fact they have been so much fun that I didn't think to keep them, discarding them as soon as the idea was exhausted. Fortunately, I purposed some of these automatics for a music project I composed, which forced me to save some of them.

It is a fun and provocative process and you are encouraged to try it out for yourself. Sit down and have at it. Let me know what you come up with.

CHAPTER 1: KAMI NO KURA

Flutterby

I will kiss your tiny wounds until the dawn and they will heal with great speed and tickle like butterfly kisses.

Alchemy Like Dirt

A ceramic cricket was found on the nap of the neck of a dead prostitute. The cause of death was never revealed. Clutched tightly in her left hand was a note concerning the same map that had been my life's work for the past twenty odd years. The connection between the girl and the map was a mystery and I wondered how many more twists I could take in my seemingly endless and futile search for this mystical diagram.

The cricket was of extraordinary quality and detail. It's exoskeleton was a high gloss pure white with exquisite and brightly colored features, not unlike a Byzantine mosaic, only far more minutely refined, like that of traditional ceramic work from Thailand.

The true wrinkle to this scene was that the cricket was real; it was alive, or at least was when the body was discovered. It seems the insect died of asphyxiation from being painted with ceramic gloss paint.

Across the Maps of Heaven

A recurring theme in dreams of mine, and one that I'm sure many of you have experienced, is where I have the ability to fly. Whether I am being chased by someone or a mob, or I just feel the need to get somewhere quickly, I find myself able to lift off of the ground, if I can concentrate hard enough, and soar above the trees.

Many times in these dreams, usually when I feel my life is in peril, it becomes difficult to focus on the ability to fly and I find myself losing altitude, or barely able to rise above the ground for more than a few yards. The pressure to be able to clearly fix my attention on how I make myself climb into the air can be overpowering and the sense that I do not quite understand how I make myself fly becomes apparent.

Other times, with deliberate clarity and pinpoint lucidity, I can fly with the precision of true creatures of the air, controlling direction, speed and accuracy. With near euphoric glee, I can see the world from 20-30 feet in the air, rise slowly behind a lamp post and notice the details of the tops of the bulb cover; the rust around the bolts, the soldering used for permanent attachment, to float above it and hover there to inspect the minor flaws and finer particulars.

But I'm sure you know exactly what I mean.

Almost Edible

I wedged a shaft of corn chip between my teeth and pressed it into my gum. The blood tasted rather sweet, not metallic as it usually did. The pain was sharper than usual and I began to see stars. A wave of nausea and overwhelm came over me and my balance failed.

Just before hitting the floor I could see the beginning of a double rainbow in the distance. The sound of trickling water and rusty hinges filled my ears as the prismatic towers began to solidify.

When I regained consciousness, I realized the double rainbows were actually two short legs wearing colorful knee-high socks. They belonged to a young girl, about six, who was standing over me with a baseball bat.

I could see the impression my head had made in the side of the aluminum slugger. It was accompanied by bits of my hair and a spattering of my blood.

"Don't ever touch my chips again," she spat at me and turned away. She really likes her corn chips, I thought as I drifted back into unconsciousness.

Omnivorous
Incantations
(of the Lesser Known)

audio snacks

      that sound delicious.
  music for closets,

aural fixation,

      chunks of sound.

  it's noisology.

        sonic ambush,

    harmonic assault.
  intonations of the sole.

  modulating circumstances.

a deep racket;
    resonant alchemy

      for bent ears.

CHAPTER 2: MIRTH

Theatre of Lost Recollection

There was a girl I used to know, who would meet me after school once every couple of weeks and we would talk about the strangest things. She did not particularly stand out in a crowd, nor was she wallpaper, but, looking back, I think I may have been in love with her.

She had experienced a life that is, to this day, unknown in origin to me, and fantastical in nature. She had lived her childhood on ocean cliffs and watched the shoreline shrink and fall into the ocean. She witnessed the winter foxes leave the earth and was the last person to hear their cries. She studied alchemy with a Middle Eastern "wise-woman", who was supposedly a direct descendant of the Witch of Endor, who summoned the spirit of the dead prophet Samuel for King Saul.

She would speak in rhymes, in a sing-songy manner that made it seem as if she was caroling her story to you, with a voice of an angel, or more accurately, a siren, creating magical and intricate weavings with her lyrical words and melodic cadence. Lost moments in the elusive arms of contentment.

One day, just before I was to graduate from university, we met in our usual place. Something had agitated her and she was distraught in appearance. She said to me, "the skies are full, they harbor all my dreams. Burst a cloud, my hopes begin to bleed." Then, without warning, she ran off. I would never see her again. I still dream of her story songs.

Darkly
Boxes

Wednesday afternoon at the cafe was the usual outing for my wife and I during times when the weather allowed for such luxuries. We would sit in the front window and have our tea, feeling rather posh and sophisticated. The view from our perch of the small but quaint downtown street corner was somewhat, "wild western", with it's raised wooden sidewalks, hitching posts for horses with accompanying trough for water, and a dry, dusty road separating the rows of rustic shops on either side.

This particular afternoon, I decided to treat myself to a scoop of ice cream, as the cafe was well known for it's abundance of flavors, although neither of us had ever tried them. I was informed by the waiter that the servings were available through the back doors and I could help myself to whatever flavor I chose. As I stood to go and explore my choices, I happened to look out of the window to see a girl, in the distance, running into town. She was too far away to make out any details, but she was wearing a pink dress with red shoes, her blonde hair pulled back into a ponytail. Something struck me as peculiar about her, but I paid it little mind as my thoughts were consumed by my consumable options.

Entering the back area, through the doorway, the lights were very dim and it took me several seconds for my eyes to adjust. Once I could see my surroundings I noticed the grounds were covered with numerous open graves, all with shovels propped up within. As I moved closer to the graves nearest me, I could see that they were filled with ice cream; hundreds of open graves filled with various ice cream, the flavor carved into the headstone associated with the grave. This was quite novel, indeed.

Looking about the space, I became excited to peruse the variety, reading the headstones to see what caught my fancy: Rum Raison, Strawberry Vanilla Walnut, Almond Chocolate, Stainless Steel, Granite, Athlete's Foot...wait, what? These were the most unorthodox flavors, and not at all appetizing... Monkey Hair, Mange, Dry Glass Sand, Old Chalk.

I had enough for today.

Returning to our table near the front window, I noticed my wife was no longer there, but was, instead, replaced by the girl wearing the pink dress and red shoes. She made no suggestion that anything had run afoul, so I, not wanting to upset the situation, pretended everything was as normal. We finished our tea and decided to take the long walk back home.

To this day, I still do not know whatever became of my wife.

A Conversation Once

I dreamt of a crow who told me it sang to you when you were a little girl. He had beautiful things to say about your childhood, although they were from the eyes of a crow.

"Did you really dream that?"

I may have, but I probable just wrote it.

"What did he say about my childhood?"

That your life was surely filled with wonder and great things were in store.

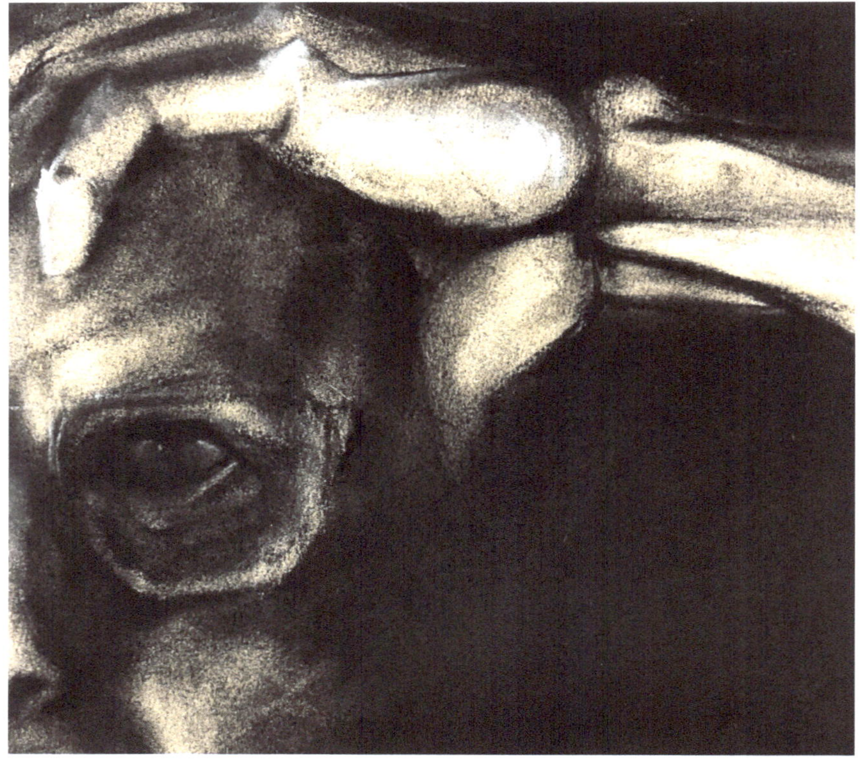

In The Form Of Working Tools

I woke up wet with sweat from the lack of a descent air conditioner unit. The windows were open, letting in the stench of the city and the rot of morning. It was my treasure hunting day. For years, I have scavenged through fields with my Symbatico 4000 deluxe metal detector, searching for anything that could be of interest or profit. Although rather fruitless, I, nonetheless, made it a weekly ritual of scouting out abandoned lots and long alleyways throughout the city. Places where the scavenging had yielded some sort of success were frequented on a regular basis. Curiously, many of these frequented locations were near where I lived. On the morning of August 11 I found a human eye in the vacant lot near my apartment building. The eyeball was fully intact and the muscles were cleanly cut, suggesting removal from the head by another person without struggle. The eye was soft and moist and unusually warm. I could feel it twitch, contracting with nerves still active. How could this be? For the eye to still be transmitting neuron signals would mean the eye was removed right there, right then. There was no evidence of foul play, no body or head nearby.

I decided to take it home for a closer look.

The room was rather warm, as most apartments on the eighth floor with fickle air conditioning tend to be, so I opened the windows wide.

Examining the eye further, I noticed the color to be exactly like my own. I noticed it twitch and felt a mild pain shoot behind my right eye.

At the same time, I heard the Symbatico 4000 turn on and emit a strange droning sound.

A booming voice greeted me and I could not tell from where the voice was coming. It seemed to be from inside my head.

"We'll need to retake that scene, Mr. Fields, please take your place."

The Symbatico lurched forward and sprouted limbs. It's upper appendages ended with clutching, finger-like mechanisms, one grabbing my arm, the other retrieving a very sharp scalpel.

Before I could make any kind of defensive move it had me wrapped up and was holding my head back. Small tentacle like branches emerged from its torso, working in unison much like centipede legs. They clung to my face forcing my eye open. The tentacles dug into my skin and attached to my skull. Pain seared through me as the fingers stretched then tore the flesh from around my eye, leaving the eyeball ready for plucking, not unlike a pistachio from its shell.

My vision was blurring as the Symbatico removed my eye and severed the muscles. As I began to black out I could hear the voice shout, "NO, not that window! Cut! Cut! We'll have to do that one again."

I woke up wet with sweat from the lack of a descent air conditioner unit. The windows were open, letting in the stench of the city and the rot of morning. It was my treasure hunting day.

Tepid Wobble

I failed to notice the red flashing lights outside of my window on the night of the incident. I had been drinking and was exaggeratedly preoccupied with a news article on social media for the warning to catch my attention. Once they burst into the room wielding their various weapons and flashlights, it was far too late for me to react.

Before I could gather my senses, I was being held face down on the floor with a man burying his knee into my back and another with a pistol to the side of my head. They claimed to be officers of the sanity division and were accusing me of having violated the local ordinances of exaggeration.

Not understanding any of this, I shouted back that they must be in the wrong place, arresting the wrong person. What had I done that was out of the ordinary, that was outrageous in any way?

After cuffing my hands the officer who was on my back, Officer Shaw, lifted me up, dusted me off, and proceeded to lecture me on the dangers of an over imaginative mind, in the wrong state. As he did so, he also informed me of my rights and what I could do for my own protection once I was released.

Still having no clue of what Officer Shaw was referring to, I baulked at the notion of going anywhere with them. He them proceeded to show me what I had done as a result of overactive dreaming, under the influence.

Escorting me into my own back bedroom, the officers flung open the door to reveal a scene chimeric.

Ancient masks were flying around the room singing Al Jolson songs as a large snail churned butter in a rusted spittoon. Fire rose and fell from burping orifices in the floor as well dressed pygmies laughed and leaped about them playing some sort of chasing game. A humanoid-like being, about seven feet tall, grabbed one of the pygmies by the feet and started slamming it over the large throne centerpiece in the room, until parts of the pygmy's body began to hurl about, causing the other pygmies to alter their game to include avoiding the dismembered segments. Children riding upon the back of a giant centipede, not unlike a small train in an amusement park, wove in and out of the gapping, belching mini-volcanoes until the 7 foot giant sliced the centipede in half, leaving the last two children sitting aboard an unmoving fragment of the ride, waving goodbye to a steamboat as it turned down the river that ran into my closet. On board was my step father and his new bride, wearing silver pajamas and matching hats.

There was Batman standing at the side of the room trying to make sense of it all, when I saw a needle rise from the ground and inject him in the leg. Writhing in pain, Batman's appearance began to change. He became grotesquely bulbous and mutated into some sort of hairless gorilla or more like a distorted, warped version of a gorilla. Showing intense hostility and rage, he noticed me and surged at me. The officers slammed shut the door just before the mutated Batman was able to grab me.

"Do you see that?!? Do you see what you've done?!? It's going to take days to clean this mess up. Now, come on, we're going to take you down to the station. What, exactly, were you drinking?"

Yes, what exactly WAS I drinking?

Scratch Apparatus

I once knew a man who liked to jab everyone with his elbow. He would do it as a friendly greeting, as a way to provoke aggression, or as a way of emphasizing a point in a conversation. He was considerably annoying and most everyone I knew made their best attempts to avoid him when he was present.

Then, one day, he approached me as I was taking an afternoon walk around the neighborhood. He again stuck out his elbow and poked me directly in the ribs. Having had enough of this irritation, I shouted for him to stop doing that. He then, with an air of sardonic authority, proceeded to illuminate the reason for this type of greeting.

"Where I come from," he grinned, "we do not have hands as you know them. Our fingers are short, stubby appendages with prickly spears along the sides. Needless to say, this makes handshaking, slapping other people on the back, and high five greetings a predicament. But for you, I'll say, good afternoon."

He grabbed my hand and an intense pain coursed through my body. How did I never notice those clawlike hands of his? Like tiny javelins, the needles punctured my hand and wrist, sinking deeply into my flesh, contacting the bone underneath.

I tried to break free, but the more I struggled to get away, the more his porcupine stranglehold kept me in place. My knees began to buckle and as I fell to the ground, I could feel a growth within my burning hand; an osmosis stemming from the spears, a transference not unlike spores.

After he let go and walked away, I hesitated before looking down at my hand. As I feared, the spear had imbedded into my hand, transforming it into a replica of his hand. The joints of my hand were stiff and rigid, not able to maneuver in the same way it had before.

So, the next time you ask me to stop jabbing you with my elbow, try not to shout at me, be less confrontational, and know that a worse fate will occur if this happens again. Good afternoon.

Theoretically

In high school, I was part of an outsider pack of friends who were not particularly liked by anyone. We were awkward, intelligent and partook in plenty of drugs and substances. The jocks of the school hated us because we were considered stoners, the stoners hated us because we were smart and threw the grading curve and the popular students just flat out hated everything about us. Needless to say, high school was not the glory days for me.

As we grew up, our pack of undesirables grew apart. As years went by, I lost track of all but one, who was fortunately in a position to give me employment, when I needed it.

After a few months working together, we were both shocked when a third person from the high school pack came through the door of the office looking for a job. He, of course, was hired, and we reconnected, the three of us, after a number of years apart.

Something had happened to our third amigo that we could not identify or assess. He behaved skittish, like an animal in danger. Finally, we had to confront him about this agitated state.

"I think I'm being followed by the CIA" he admitted. "It's been like this for a few weeks."

Trying not to laugh and be mocking, we asked, "Why on earth would the CIA be following you?"

"I've discovered how to extract gold from salt water," he blurted out. "This happened while I was in exile on an island off French Guiana." We, of course, found this preposterous and somewhat deranged. Worried that it may cause a problem, I quickly changed the subject and we moved on with the conversation to more conventional subject matters.

We would never see him again. He would never show up again for work, his phone was disconnected and there was never again any trace of him ever coming back into our lives. To this day, I wonder if he actually figured out the gold extraction, and what could possibly be the interest in this discovery for the CIA.

CHAPTER 3: THE SCIENCE OF OBSCURITY

Feathers From Unused Wings

A bird had unexpectedly found its way on bus #17 and was unable to find a way out. In a state of panic, it flew full speed toward the open sky outside the closed window. Broken, it fell dead to the floor of the bus near her. She watched it all happen. She noticed the way the limp body of the bird lay there. She noticed the blood stain on the window at eye level. She noticed the loosened feathers being pushed about by the air conditioning system of the bus. She noticed it all as the bus made its route to her workplace. And then she noticed it as the bus pulled away from her bus stop. She did not move. She did not blink. Bus #17 continued along its scheduled route. And time passed.

She had been staring at the dead bird for several days. It was a cardinal, at one time. A fierce intensity surrounded her and the others could not penetrate this barrier. She had isolated herself within this cocooning trance and had forced her focus so intently upon the carcass that nothing could distract her.

No one knows exactly why she was left in her seat. No one really noticed her, at first. She became a part of bus #17. Every so often the others would try to catch her attention, ask her if she was okay, or nudge her gently. Once, some teenagers spray painted across her right arm, but even that act received no notice.

For a time, the others continued to try to rouse her from this catatonic state with food, pleas, as well as threats, but to no avail. At that point they surrendered to the situation and decided to wait it out. And bus #17 kept to its scheduled route.

Within her consciousness, She was vaguely aware of what was happening around her. The intention was to keep all of it outside of her concentration so she could operate, with pinpoint precision, her transformation. Deeper and stronger her focus became, overwhelming what was once the limits of her being, taking her far beyond her own existence.

For several months She had struggled within the confines of her life, unable to let go of her past burdens. She wore them as a badge while using them as her crutch. Feathers from unused wings. They were her excuses for giving up, for not trying harder, for letting things pass.

Yet they were put on display not unlike a treasured artifact in a museum. Her association with her burdens was so cemented as her comfort barrier that it became who she was and she no longer thought of working to fix or eliminate them. She wore them as identities, sliding them on as skins, and assuming them as inevitable.

This affected her life in the present and she allowed it to. There was one who loved her and whom she once loved, but the happiness they brought each other did not fit into the creation of who she was becoming. He had been the driver of bus #17 for many years. It was how they met, being that bus #17 was the bus that routed her to her work. But after a while she felt need for separation and distance. She would avoid him for long periods of time just to make sure she kept enough distance, that there was enough separation between them for her burdens to grow. And, although this was surely taking its toll, he stuck by her even during the most trying times. She would ride bus #17 to work without saying a word to him. She would sit in her seat and avoid his glances. After a while he too stopped noticing. After a time, he no longer was the driver of bus #17.

It may have been that She thought this was personal growth, that by allowing her burdens to take over, she was confronting them. She may have believed them to be placed upon her by others, that she was not responsible for them and that she could do nothing about them. This would certainly strengthen her belief that she was not responsible for what they did to her or to others. She may even have believed the best course of action was no action; that in order to overcome your burdens you just have to wait them out and they will become more and more transparent, until they are no longer seen, until they could fly. Discarded angels.

The others set about continuing their lives, doing what they could to make sure she was not forgotten or neglected. As time passed, however, less and less thought was given to the girl on the bus transfixed upon the dead bird until she was no more regarded than an overlooked pile of leaves or a discarded soda can. That was when she succeeded. It was at that moment the transformation took place.

She lifted her head and shook off the debris that had collected upon her. Looking around she was quite aware of how quickly her head moved as she scanned the surroundings. She tried to call out but a horrible, gurgling sound came up from her throat and panic started to set in. The mechanics within her didn't seem right, She felt as though her insides were churned and altered. She was acutely aware of her small size and vulnerable location. Anxiety to reach a high vantage point took over and she thought it best to take action. She spread her matted wings and attempted to gain height. It took several attempt to get her wings unstuck from her body, they had been flattened together for so long. It took much longer for her to figure out how to work her new body so she remained hidden in dark corners under the seats.

The others did not know how long it had been since the girl in the seat had disappeared. The first one who noticed walked past where she had been, nearly tripping on the tattered blanket left to warm her during colder nights, before realizing her absence. His startled gestures drew attention to the situation and soon several of the others were standing about the seat of the missing girl, searching for clues. The one thing they all could not escape was the unusual song coming from beneath the seats. "Is that a bird?" "What kind of bird could that be?" "I've never heard anything sound like that before."

She took flight, not sure of her abilities or how to make adjustments. Through intense concentration she was able to control her speed and direction, but it was clumsy and awkward, like a first bicycle ride.

Panic hit the others as they scrambled to open windows to allow the bird to escape. She, too, was full of frenzy and confusion, seeking only to gain freedom, to enter the endless sky. Finding an open window she dashed through and felt an enormous expansion of air. This is what it was like to be without burden, to be free of their prison.

With her focus so fixated upon her movements, she was not aware of the large object approaching behind her. By the time she noticed, it was too late.

"God damn bird," shouted the bus driver as a loud thud echoed through the cabin. The windshield wipers were unable to clear off all the blood and a bright red feather hung from the rattling wiper blade as it screeched it's way across the front window. Bus #17 would be slightly delayed.

Albatross Alacrity

I found the remains of an unknown type of animal once. The pelvic bone was split, not broken. Stemming from the left side of the pelvic region was what looked like a second head or possibly some sort of tumor that had ruptured. The creature had been dead a while but was not completely decomposed. It had not flattened, but was still stiffened

from rigor mortis. I took a stick and, thinking it would be a funny prank to passers by, lifted it up so it would stand on it's hind legs. This took several attempts to succeed as the position of the body was not very balanced. To my surprise, as soon as it balanced upright, the animal turned it's head, looked me square in the face, winked, and darted off into the woods.

Damnedest thing I ever saw.

CHAPTER 4: CYCAURUS

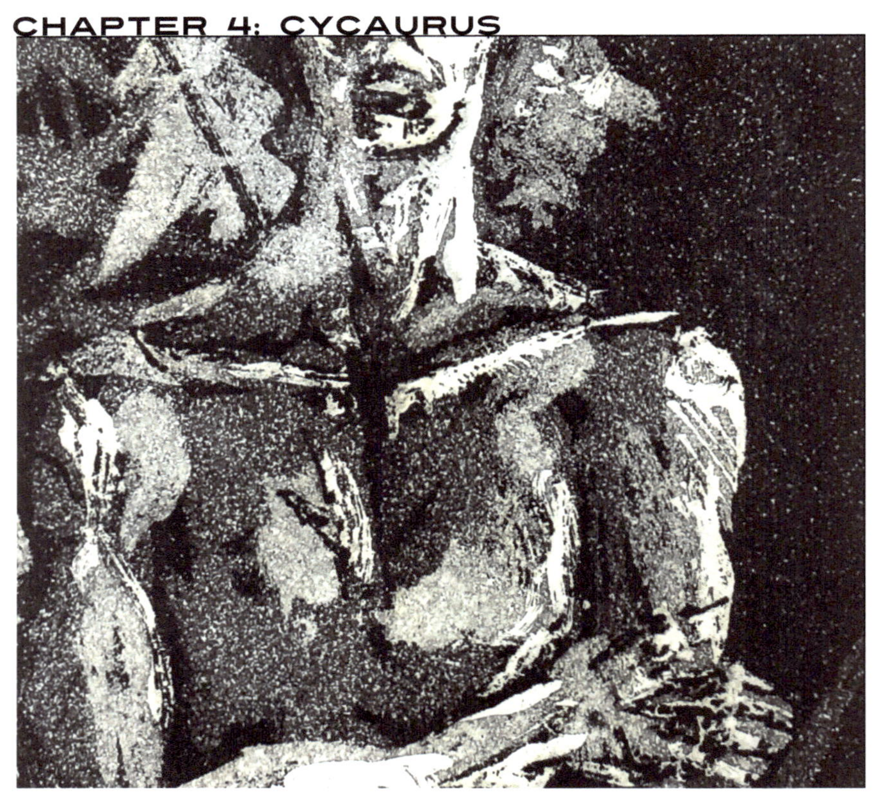

Cycaurus
in four parts

I.

The laureate suffers
the fate of the
addict when faced with
fruitful condemnation.

"Subtilty in retrospect,"
the heretic bellows
froth from his makeshift
alter. Creeps forth.

Consoling laborous hatred;
clings to the fettered
carcass of love.
Shrivelled deformity of
life long neglect
that wades through pools
of urine, stench of defecation.

Destined as the only retreat.
Shelters the honor of thieves
and lunatic desire.

It is in the bowels of the
serpent I find you, Cycaurus,
lover of all but one.

You weep, but your
words, like futile insects,
are caught in the throat
of the new born.

II.

I whisper words of enchantment
that ghost the image of Cycaurus
and echo the covenant of Pan.
Desire unfolds to touch
your golden mane and
audience the unvailing
of the virgin.

You receive my message
with the langer of superiority.
showing truths behind masks
of infatuation; the fetish of fools.

Sing to me —
The showers of evenings
lost with time/
revealed in slumber/
and salted with age.

To seek refuge in the
domain you have shown.

Me — distilled and abiding —
the simple solace of love
shimmers in the hands
romance has held for us.

III.

The days
flow of skillful
patience serving
requiem.
Forgotten heros
Sing cold fevered
sun cast abandon
from within these
halls; I suffer
the fate of
ill-repute and
vouch for the
honor of saints,
who beware my
presence with a
vengeance I had not
forseen — Shivering rot
in explanation of the
death of Cycaurus,
a dear friend and lover,
I feast upon his flesh
sweet – infested lust
of a soul that
remained unturned.

IV.

Cycaurus of Klee,
rebute my claim
of significance.
We devour multitudes,
we seek darkness.
Rejoicing footfalls
of humiliation that
asunder upon command;
to share in ritual
digression.

...showing bones
of confusion.

...leading torrents
of rage.

Strike —

leash out upon
the mother of
patience.
Feel flesh,
tear paper sinew,
and hold her carcass;
child of
forbidden love.

September 28

Feeble wisps of wind
maze through her silken hair;
dark, unending mane
now tangled and manged,
reaching to choke me.
Vengeful mystery motive.
My hands frail and decomposing;
earthly canvas fester,
longing to hold her once more.
Ages since last we met.
flickering blue diamond
fading crushed hollow
to know she no longer
wants me, laughs
as my knees collapse,
concealing bastard faults
that hasten one's longing
to part.
To nurse upon the nipple
of the rotting animal;
gangrenous array love.
Sore ridden profile.
I shall leave not
knowing why I stayed.
Death spits love,
a curious thing.

October 25

An autumn unexpected
filters
the marrow of winter;
hangs heavy
as scent of flesh
and warmth of moisture.

He entertain contempt
and guarded treasure.
Softly comfort
drains as concubine
feast — nurture.

Save the boy
of the fallen mane.
Wounded deep / scarred tissue,
and drink from the well,
the girl of sunlight.

February 12

Softly,
a breeze engulfs me
with feverish delight.
To contemplate
upon my stance
The bliss of golden mane
splashes about me
in nymphatic dances
and speculate upon
this desire unrestrained.
Fanciness once broken
now adopts
to a new order;
challenges the foes of Aphrodite.
Beguiled pleasures
I had not known
before;
and I no longer
wonder where the
days go to rest.

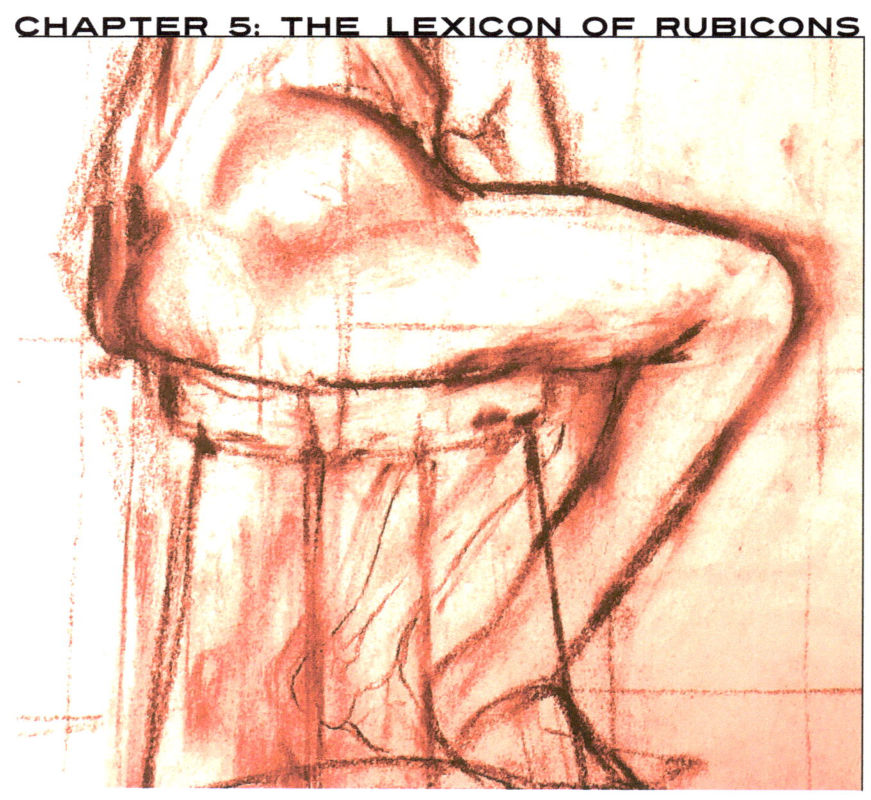

Oscar

When I was a kid, about six, I had a pet toad named Oscar. Oscar would live in my shirt pocket and we would go on long bike rides and climb trees. One day I was very high up in a tree and Oscar decided to explore. Not being a frog, he immediately plummeted to the ground. Panicked, I climbed down as fast as I could only to find Oscar, quite shaken, smoking a cigarette. I told him to stop smoking. He told me to fuck off.

Delirium Failure

When I was about four or five years old I was convinced I could defy the laws of physical nature, if I could concentrate hard enough and focus my willpower sharply enough. I had visions of what I could do but they only appeared to me as daydreams. Then one day, early afternoon in autumn, I did it. I was able to overcome physical limitations and I became omnipresent. It only lasted for a second or two but I will never forget that feeling. I could feel myself expanding out, beyond the boundaries of what I could physically see, beyond the land, the oceans, the stars. Beyond the universe and beyond my own awareness. I woke up in the emergency ward. Apparently, I had suffered a seizure. A brood vessel had burst in my brain. Was it the vision that caused the seizure or the other way around?

The Flat Ironed Earth

I startled myself awake: groggy and dehydrated. As disoriented as I was, I realized very quickly that I was in a hospital bed and it appeared to be in a long term facility. Expensive medical instrumentation, hibernating and unused, surrounded me.

Something was slowly moving above the television set. It was a small human-like creature made of solid rock. It moved with great effort and was somewhat awkward, as if not used to having to engage in motion. I checked to see that there were no cartoons playing on the tv that would be an obvious reason for this delusion. Nope, no cartoons.

He called himself a stone guy and with his accent, somewhat Asian in nature, it sounded cute. He then smiles at me, relaxing my anxious hesitancy which, I'm sure, covered my face.

Looking around the dimly lit room, I noticed there were more of them, sitting on the side table, the shelves and the unused instrumentation.

I felt they were there for me, and me alone. It was as if they were there to greet me as I awakened.

Out of the corner of my eye, I saw one of these stone creatures leap from his perch and land on my leg, crushing the bones inside.

Again and again, others would fall on me damaging me immensely and flattening that part of my body.

As they threw themselves at me, the stone guys would crumble into rubble, in the form of kamikaze suicide missions.

Curiously, I felt no pain at all. It was a little disconcerting, but it actually felt rather pleasant, one after the other, pummeling my flesh.

I saw in their eyes that this was a sacred ritual, and that I should be honored to have been chosen.

Was I still asleep and dreaming?

Melanie, a first year care nurse, had just arrived at the hospital for her shift. She had not had a very eventful weekend and was annoyed that she had left her prepared lunch on the kitchen counter at home. Walking through the front doors she noticed a commotion.

How could this have happened?

It seems a John Doe who was left here in a comma 8 month ago, had just passed away. However, the circumstances were most peculiar. It seems he was discovered crushed and flat as a pancake, appearing a bit cartoonish and comical, as if the victim in a Tex Avery nightmare. The cadaver could be folded like washed sheets or an old flag. It certainly made it easy to dispose of the remains.

And yet, still no cartoons on the television.

what if...

What if god did exist and he actually did all the things that were written about him concerning the creation of, well, everything, but due to the stress mankind has forced upon him, the utter humiliation of things done in his name, the misuse of his teachings for personal agendas and greed, the selfish prayer demands, the inhumanity that his creations have perpetrated and rote upon itself; he suffers from PTSD. The lord is overcome with anxiety and depression, and can no longer function properly. And even though he makes attempts to prove that he is there and is real, the contact is feeble and forgettable due to his lack of willpower. The flickering of lights in the bathroom, the flat tire that made you late to work, the missing left sock... the best he could do. What if god can only communicate with color and we've misinterpreted the messages? He reaches out for our help, for our understanding, for our compassion, and no one notices, at all. His pleas are merely paint and decor to us. He is utterly alone, more alone than we could ever imagine. He is as a teenager who has been bullied to his limit. So, where does this go? What would happen if a god committed suicide? What would happen if a god snapped, took an assault rifle into a school, so to speak? I'm guessing we may soon find out.

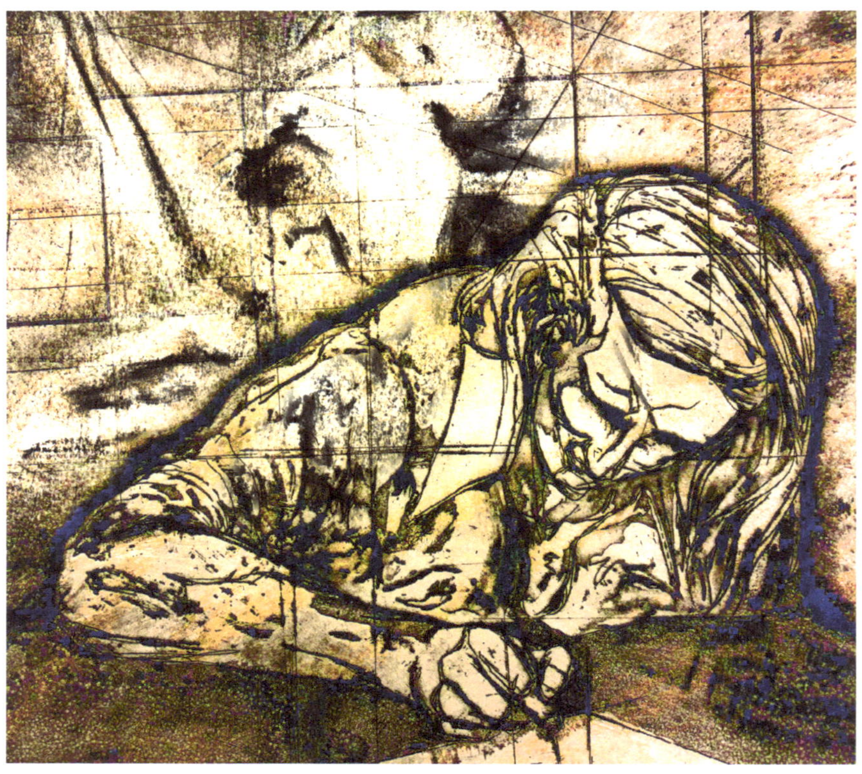

Cowboy & Indian

I am standing by a barbed wire fence, my hand resting on the wooden post near the gate. I look over the field at the mountain range looming over the land.

I stand by the fence, my hand resting on the post while twilight casts its misty gaze upon the valley I am overlooking.

I am near the gate, my hand resting, waiting for nightfall as the shadow of the mountains fade into the colors of dusk settling on the field in the valley I look upon.

This moment is endless, an infinite sequence of lifetimes that pass before my watchful eyes, as I stand by the fence, my hand resting on the post, seeking the solace of dark evenings that never arrive.

52nd and Third

It happened at precisely 3:52pm on a bright, yet moderate, Sunday afternoon at the corner of 52nd and Third, immediately outside the old fourth-generation-Vietnamese-owned corner convenient store. The incident was miraculously captured by 43 people, in addition to 4 street monitoring devices. These evidence-gathering instruments ranged in resolution quality from pixilated photos on outdated cellphones to high end digital cameras with telephoto lenses, even an antiquated video camcorder. The documentation of evidence was staggering.

Although each of these observational tools recorded the exact same moment at the exact same location, all were from vastly different perspectives and viewpoints from around the city block. Strangely, every single one of them had vastly different recollections of what they had chronicled. It was as if, given the same set of circumstances and subjects, each witness created their own situation and event.

The bewildering aspect of this quandary was that none of the eyewitnesses could even come close to corroborating, or even resembling, the story of another. Not a single one.

The photographs and videos were examined repeatedly, and not only were the accounts by the people vastly disparate, the captured images showed completely contrasting events, all involving the same subject, at the same moment, in the same environment. In fact, more often than not, they were contradicting previous attestation.

No one knew what to do about it.

I thought about this a long time before taking another bite of my sandwich.

Like Tears In Rain

I keep thinking about the monologue near the end of the film *Bladerunner*, where Rutger Hauer, as the replicant Roy Batty, is dying in the rain on the rooftop, talking about how all of his extraordinary experiences will be forever lost.

"All those moments will be lost in time, like tears in rain. Time to die."

And then I personalize this poignant thought and realize there are so many things I've seen and experienced that only I have known. That are so uniquely mine, alone. So much witnessed that I rarely share with any other soul.

Expanding this thought outside of my personal universe, I realize, all of us, every single person, everyone you've ever met in your life, has their own remarkable and anomalous moments in their own life that only they have known.

So many moments of brilliance to share, but they are precious in their divinity. They are very exploitable, fragile, and are susceptible to profanation, to be made ordinary, if used inappropriately.

I realize these are the sparks of life that we share in moments of exceptional closeness. These sparks are to be used sparingly. They are not the photos in Facebook posts. They are not your personal perspective on social media comments. They are not the stories we share with boisterous pride in large gatherings. They are not the tall tales we associate with one another. They are gifts we share when the moment calls for it. They offer a unique connection with the one you share it with.

"All those moments will be lost in time..."

So, honor your spark. Keep them sacred. Realize just how special they are. And share your spark, but share them wisely.

CHAPTER 5: THE LEXICON OF RUBICONS

ADDENDUM

Included in this addendum are the instructions for two of the musical pieces I've created using similar techniques to Automatics, or that actually used the Automatics within the pieces.

Feel free to use these instructions, if you wish, in your own explorations.

Pisang Zapra

Performed by the Tangled Bell Ensemble.

*The first incarnation of this piece was titled Midaregami (Tangled Hair)
and used the tanka poetry of Akiko Yosano.*

The main goal of this exploration is to juxtapose seemingly conflicting concepts and approaches, and display them in an aligning way; to show how antagonistic forces and unfamiliarity can create a cooperative friction and become formidable allies. The intent being that all portions of the whole (notated music, text, improvisation) were at once independent of and mutually dependent upon each other; symbiotic; each being a part and apart simultaneously.

By coordinating loosely written themes that rely on improvisation for story detail, the inclusion of musicians with vast differences in musical background and influence, semi-spontaneous arrangements and impromptu conducting, Pisang Zapra is presented as more of an experimental "state of the union" than a completed work.

Creating an environment where the construction of composition is immediate and experientially apparent has been an objective of mine for some time. The game piece, Milton Bradley (2012), attempted to coax improvisors into immediate composers by interpretation.

The Dada poetry of Tristan Tzara shows its influence in this piece of music in two ways.

First, through the words themselves; poignant and clever, sharp and witty, dark and humorous, deconstructive and fluid, all at once. Getting to the point was not the end goal, but was part of the process.

Also influencing the music is the rhythm and phrasing of Tzara's poetry; very musical but very non-Western and collage-like. As with most stream of consciousness writing and use of "cut-up" or random phrasing within a context, many times the gist of a paragraph or work will not present itself entirely until late or even at the end of the piece. The idea is not realized until completed.

Juxtaposition is used between the words of Tzara and my own personal "responses", both in words and sound. This is meant not so much as a call and response, but rather like a conceptual "inside/outside" viewpoint of the same situation.

I am extremely honored to share this journey with the musicians here. Each of these performers brings vast knowledge from vary diverse spectrums of the musical universe.

Milton Bradley

Written for a performance in Jacksonville, FL marking the
100th birthday of John Cage.

Milton Bradley is a chance operation piece based on the structure and advancement techniques used in family board games. The full description of the operation is "chance operation within finite parameters using board game mechanics resulting in instant compositions." Rules and parameters are followed in order much the same way as board game participation.

Participants are positioned around a table. Before commencement, the players have selected three instruments and placed each in separate groups: Blue, Red, or Yellow, with Blue being their primary instrument.

I. The first player to take their turn is the *leader* and spins the dial. The dial is an eight section spin dial.

The dial will determine the number of participants to play on this particular piece. The spinner will land on either solo, duo, trio, quartet, leader decides, high roller decides, exquisite corpse, or lecture bowl.

• Solo, duo-right, duo-left, trio, and quartet are self-explanatory and the participants are chosen by the leader.

• Leader decides: the player in charge determines how many and who is playing that piece.

• Exquisite corpse: All players will perform but will play one at a time, beginning with the leader, moving right to left. Each player will continue from the previous players end point, which will be random and determined by the players themselves.

• Lecture bowl: The leader determines the instrumentation to accompany them as they read from the cut-up strips of text from the bowl. The text is drawn from instructions of actual Milton Bradley games and from the text of John Cage's Intermediacy stories.

2. The leader rolls large die. This will determine length of piece, from one to six minutes.

3. The leader draws a card from the deck.

This will determine what is to be interpreted. This may be either a style description, a photograph, a drawing, an emotion, a situation, or the interpretation of a graphic score. The interpretation of the card is completely up to the leader of the piece and any instructions to the participants is allowed *before* commencing the piece.

• If a graphic score card is drawn, the graphic score can be divided up, sectioned, and designated by the leader in any way they wish.

4. Finally, the leader will select a color tile. Tile will be selected from the grab bag. This will determine instrumentation.

- Blue: Primary instrument of participant
- Red: Secondary instrument
- Yellow: Third instrument option
- Green: Leaders choice. Leader will select
  the instrumentation for participants.
- Black: Participants will select their own
  instruments to play in the piece.

5. Timer will be set for the minutes determined in step 2. When leader is ready to begin, they will start the timer. Buzzer will designate the end of the piece.

6. Player to the right will be the next leader.